HEATHER HAS
TWO MOMMIES

HEATHER HAS TWO MOMMIES

10TH ANNIVERSARY EDITION

Written by Lesléa Newman
Illustrated by Diana Souza

ALYSON
WONDERLAND

Children's Books by Lesléa Newman

PICTURE BOOKS
Matzo Ball Moon
Remember That
Saturday Is Pattyday
Thea's Throw
Too Far Away to Touch

YOUNG ADULT NOVELS
Fat Chance

Manufactured in the United States of America.
Printed on acid-free paper.

The Tenth Anniversary Edition of this Alyson Wonderland book is published simultaneously
in hardcover and paperback by Alyson Publications,
P.O. Box 4371, Los Angeles, California 90078-4371.
Distribution in the United Kingdom by Turnaround Publisher Services Ltd.,
Unit 3 Olympia Trading Estate, Coburg Road, Wood Green, London N22 6TZ England.

First edition published by In Other Words Publishing: December 1989
First Alyson Wonderland edition: June 1990
Second edition (Tenth Anniversary Edition): June 2000

00 01 02 03 04 ❖ 10 9 8 7 6 5 4 3 2 1

ISBN 1-55583-543-0 (PAPERBACK) • ISBN 1-55583-570-8 (HARDCOVER)
(Previously published with ISBN 0-06922789-0-4 by In Other Words Publishing and
with ISBN 1-55583-180-X by Alyson Publications.)

Library of Congress Cataloging-in-Publication Data
Newman, Lesléa.
Heather has two mommies / written by Lesléa Newman ; illustrated by Diana Souza—2nd ed.
Summary: When Heather goes to playgroup, at first she feels bad because she has two mothers
and no father, but then she learns that there are lots of different kinds of families and
the most important thing is that all the people love each other.
ISBN 1-55583-543-0 — ISBN 1-55583-570-8
[1. Lesbians—Fiction. 2. Gay parents—Fiction. 3. Mothers and daughters—Fiction.
4. Family—Fiction.] I. Souza, Diana, ill. II. Title
PZ7.N47988 He 2000
[Fic]—dc21   99-087285

Credits
An earlier version of the author's afterword first appeared in the March/April 1997 issue of *The Horn Book.*

For Sarah and Miranda Crane and all of their friends

HEATHER HAS
TWO MOMMIES

Heather lives in a little house with a big apple tree in the front yard and lots of tall grass in the backyard.

Heather's favorite number is two. She has two arms, two legs, two eyes, two ears, two hands, and two feet. She also has two pets: a ginger-colored cat named Gingersnap and a big black dog named Midnight.

Heather also has two mommies: Mama Jane and Mama Kate.

Mama Kate is a doctor. Heather likes to listen to her heartbeat with a real stethoscope. When Mama Kate has a headache, Heather gives her two aspirin to make her feel better. When Heather has a cut on her knee, Mama Kate puts two bandages on it.

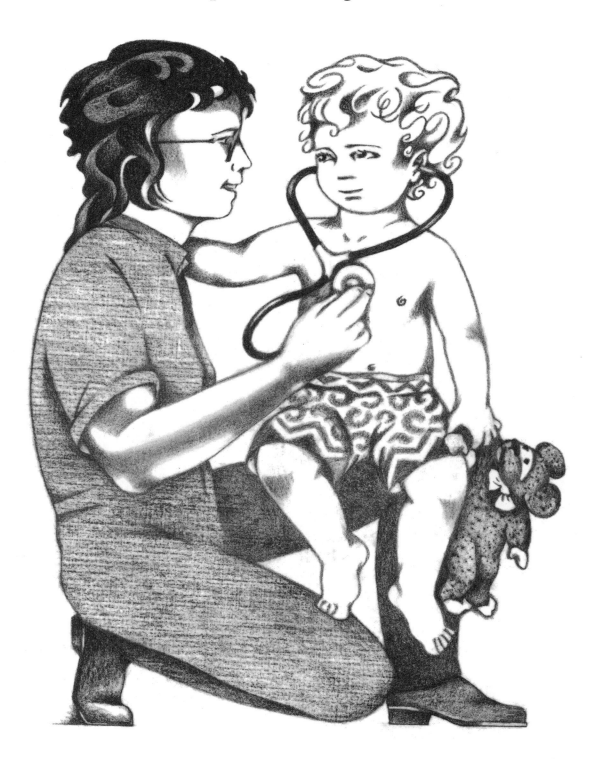

Mama Jane is a carpenter. Heather likes to look in her toolbox, where she finds nails and screws and a long yellow tape measure. Mama Jane has two hammers: a big one for herself and a little one for Heather.

On weekends Heather and her two mommies spend lots of time together. On sunny days they go to the park. On rainy days they stay inside and bake cookies. Heather likes to eat two gingersnaps and drink a big glass of milk.

One day Mama Kate and Mama Jane tell Heather they have a surprise for her. "You're going to be in a play group," Mama Kate says.

"With lots of other kids and a teacher named Molly," Mama Jane says.

"Can Midnight and Gingersnap come too?" Heather asks.

"No, they have to stay home," Mama Jane says.

"But you can bring two special things with you," says Mama Kate.

Heather picks out her favorite blue blanket to sleep with at nap time and her favorite red cup to drink out of at lunchtime.

The next day Mama Kate and Mama Jane take Heather to Molly's house.

Molly has lots of fun things to play with: books and puzzles, crayons and paint, building blocks and dress-up clothes. There's a big round table where Heather can eat her lunch and a quiet corner where Heather can take her nap. While Mama Jane and Mama Kate talk to Molly, Heather puts two puzzles together all by herself.

Soon the other children come, and it's time for Mama Jane and Mama Kate to leave. They kiss Heather good-bye, and Heather cries. But only a little.

When Heather's at Molly's house she builds a big tower out of building blocks and gets all dressed up like a firefighter. She paints two pictures at the easel—one for Mama Jane and one for Mama Kate. She drinks apple juice out of her favorite red cup at lunchtime, and she sleeps in the quiet corner with her favorite blue blanket at nap time.

After nap time, everyone sits in a circle, and Molly reads them a story about a little boy whose father is a veterinarian. He takes care of dogs and cats and birds and fish and hamsters when they get sick.

"My daddy is a doctor, too," Juan says, pointing at the book. "He takes care of sick people."

"My daddy is a teacher," David says. "Once I went to his school with him."

"I don't have a daddy," Heather says. She'd never thought about it before. Did everyone except Heather have a daddy? Heather's forehead crinkles up, and she begins to cry.

Molly picks up Heather and gives her a hug. "Not everyone has a daddy," Molly says. "You have two mommies. That's pretty special. Miriam doesn't have a daddy either. She has a mommy and a baby sister. That's pretty special too."

"I don't have any mommies. I have two daddies," Stacy says proudly.

"I have two daddies too," Joshua says. "My mommy and my stepdaddy live in a blue house, and my daddy lives by himself in a yellow house."

"Let's all draw pictures of our families," Molly says. The children all sit at the big round table, and Molly hands out paper and crayons.

Juan has a mommy and a daddy and a big brother named Carlos.

Miriam's mommy is pushing her baby sister on a swing in the park.

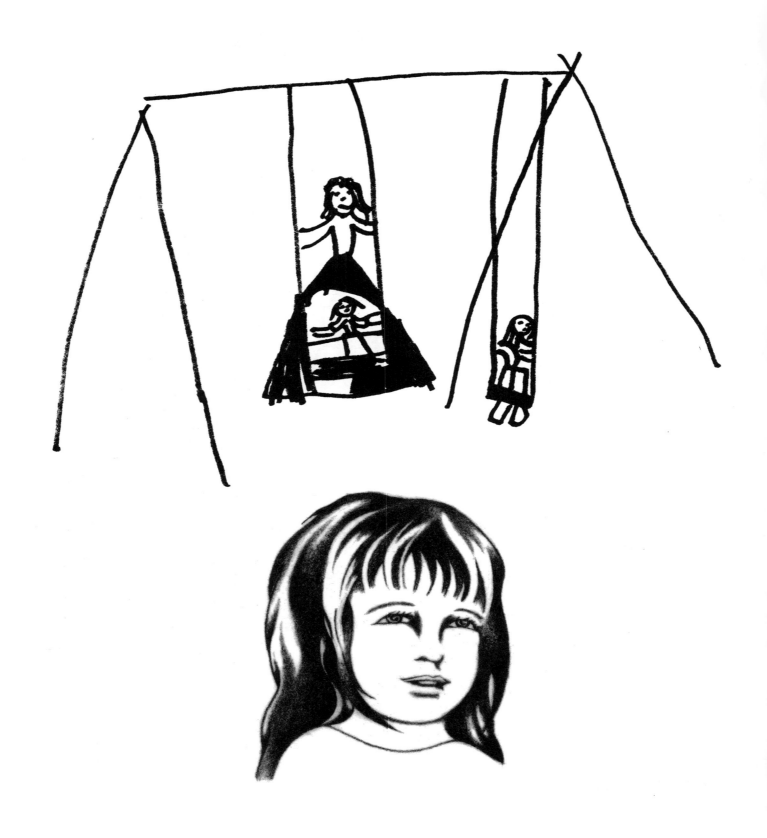

Stacy likes to sit between her two daddies on the big red couch in their living room and listen to a story.

Joshua's mommy and stepfather are dropping him off at his daddy's house.

David's mommy and daddy adopted him, his two brothers, and his big sister.

Molly hangs up all the pictures, and everyone looks at them. "It doesn't matter how many mommies or how many daddies your family has," Molly says to the children. "It doesn't matter if your family has sisters or brothers or cousins or grandmothers or grandfathers or uncles or aunts. Each family is special. The most important thing about a family is that all the people in it love each other."

Soon Heather's mommies come to take her home. Gingersnap and Midnight come too. First Heather shows them all the pictures.

"Is that me?" Mama Kate asks, pointing at Heather's picture.

"And is that me?" Mama Jane asks, pointing too.

"This is the mommy I love the best," Heather says, pointing to the mommy who has big round glasses just like Mama Kate. "And this is the mommy I love the best," Heather says, pointing to the mommy who has short red hair just like Mama Jane.

Mama Kate and Mama Jane both laugh and give Heather a great big hug. Heather gives each of her mommies two kisses before she takes their hands and heads for home.

Lesléa Newman is the author of many children's books, including *Too Far Away to Touch*, *Saturday Is Pattyday*, and *Thea's Throw*. Her literary awards include the Highlights for Children Fiction Writing Award and a Parents' Choice silver medal.

MARY VAZQUEZ

Diana Souza illustrates and designs for authors and publishers throughout the nation. Her art flows from the joy of an open heart. She lives and works wherever dreams call and dares all people to love each other and stay in tune with the soul.

Afterword: A Note to Parents and Teachers

As the author of *Heather Has Two Mommies*, I have been called the most dangerous writer living in America today. When I wrote the book, in 1988, I had no idea it would ever get published, let alone become one of the most challenged books of the 1990s. Though I have been repeatedly accused of having a militant, political agenda, my goal in writing the book was, simply, to tell a story.

The idea for *Heather* came about one day when I was walking down Main Street in Northampton, Mass., a town known for its liberalism, tolerance of difference, and large lesbian population. On this particular day I ran into a woman who, along with her female partner, had recently welcomed a child into their home. "We have no books to read our daughter that show our type of family," the woman said. "Somebody should write one."

Well, I thought, *I'm somebody. Somebody who knows firsthand what it's like to grow up without seeing families just like her own in books, in films, or on TV.* I grew up in a Jewish family, in a Jewish neighborhood. I was surrounded by families that looked like my family, families that dressed in similar clothes, families that ate similar foods. Yet I asked my parents over and over, "Why can't we have a Christmas tree? Why can't I hunt for Easter eggs?" Since I had never read a book or seen a TV show or movie about a young Jewish girl with frizzy brown hair eating matzo ball soup with her *bubbe* on a Friday night, I was convinced there was something wrong with my family. My family didn't look like any of the families I saw in my picture books or on my television set. My family was different. My family was wrong.

Of course, as a child, I was not aware of the power of the media. I was not aware of this yearning to see a family like my own reflected in the culture at large. Nor could I articulate this need. As a grown woman who happens to be a Jewish lesbian, I am painfully aware of the lack of positive images or even any images of myself in the media. I believe that had I had those images and role models at an early age, the experience would have greatly enhanced my self-esteem.

And so I took on the challenge of writing *Heather Has Two Mommies*, my only goal being to create a book that would help children with lesbian mothers feel good about themselves and their family.

I sent *Heather* to over 50 publishers. Children's book presses told me to try lesbian publishers. Lesbian publishers told me to try children's book presses. When a whole year had gone by with no luck, Tzivia Gover, a friend who is a lesbian mother, and I decided to publish the book ourselves. We sent out a fund-raising letter, promising a copy of the book in exchange for a donation of $10 or more. Four thousand dollars later, my theory was proven: There was an enthusiastic audience out there, eager for a book that displayed a child and her two lesbian mothers in a positive way.

In December of 1989 the first copies of *Heather Has Two Mommies* rolled off the presses. There wasn't a huge reaction to the book. I got a few letters from lesbian mothers telling me how grateful they were and one letter from a six-year-old named Tasha, who wrote, "Thank you for writing *Heather Has Two Mommies.* I know that you wrote it JUST FOR ME!" I heard about a little boy who received three copies of the book for his birthday and slept with all of them under his pillow every night. I also spoke with a heterosexual woman whose child was enthralled with the book. "He asks to hear it every night," she told me, "and he wants to know why he only has one mom." A sophisticated child who lives with her lesbian mom and her mom's partner asked, "How come Heather has two mommies, and I have one mommy and one parent?" Another child with two moms was completely nonplussed about the whole thing. When his mothers read him the book and asked him what he thought, he simply said, "Can we get a dog and a cat, like Heather?" I have not yet heard of a child having an adverse reaction to the book. Adults, however are another story.

In 1990 Alyson Publications started Alyson Wonderland, a line of books for children with gay and lesbian parents. Alyson bought out the rights to *Heather* and also published *Daddy's Roommate.* The books got a little more publicity at that time, but all remained quiet until 1992, when three major conflicts arose surrounding *Heather* and *Daddy's Roommate.*

The first conflict occurred in Portland, Ore., where Lon Mabon had launched an anti-gay campaign, trying to amend the state constitution to allow discrimination against lesbians and gay men. During meetings of his organization, the Oregon Citizens Alliance, copies of *Heather* and *Daddy's Roommate* were passed around as evidence of "the militant homosexual agenda" Mabon felt was sweeping the nation. On November 3, 1992, citizens of Oregon voted, and the OCA measure was defeated.

The second controversy surrounding *Heather Has Two Mommies* and *Daddy's Roommate* took place in school and public libraries around the country. As if there were a concerted effort, the books began disappearing from library shelves from coast to coast. When Alyson Publications learned of this, the company offered to send replacement copies to the first 500 libraries that called. Almost as soon as word went out, 500 calls came in. Librarians for the most part rallied around the books and defended freedom of expression as a vital principle upon which this country is based. Some libraries moved the books to the adult section, and some libraries put the books in a special request section. However, by and large, *Heather* and *Daddy's Roommate* remained on the shelves.

I was and continue to be amazed by all this fuss. It seems to me that a disproportionate number of parents live in fear of their child's reading just one book with a gay character in it, for such exposure will, in these parents' minds, cause their child to grow up to be lesbian or gay. It is usually useless to point out that the vast majority of lesbians and gay men have been brought up by heterosexual parents and spent countless hours of their childhood reading hundreds of books about heterosexual characters. Fear is an irrational thing.

The third controversy took place in New York City, around the Rainbow Curriculum, a 443-page bibliography that was designed to teach respect for all types of families. In these 443 pages, three paragraphs mention books with gay characters and themes. These books were not required to be taught or read in the classroom. They, along with hundreds of other books, were merely suggestions.

School Chancellor Joseph Fernandez was a staunch supporter of the Rainbow Curriculum. In a New York *Daily News* interview dated September 6, 1992, he said, "If we're ever going to get this country together, we have to deal with these issues of hate. Kids learn biases from us, from adults. We have to teach them tolerance through education."

Unfortunately, many people did not agree with Chancellor Fernandez, including Mary Cummins, president of School District 24 in Queens. In an interview with New York *Newsday* dated April 23, 1992, she said the Rainbow Curriculum "says teachers must tell children that all families are not heterosexual. We can't do that in the first grade." And why not, I wonder? Why not teach children in the first grade, or any other grade, the truth?

After a long and bitter battle, the Rainbow Curriculum was amended, and *Heather Has Two Mommies* and *Daddy's Roommate* were removed from its pages. For those who do not want children exposed to this type of family, I ask this: How can you possibly assume that every child sitting in your classroom or library comes from a home with a mother and father? How can you presume that there are no children in your classroom or library with lesbian or gay parents, siblings, aunts, uncles, grandparents, neighbors, and friends? What messages are you giving to all children when you pretend there is only one type of family and render the rest invisible?

All children, including children of lesbian and gay parents, will only benefit as more books on the subject of diversity get published. In the words of two such (grown) children, Stefan Lynch and Emily Omerek, codirectors of COLAGE (Children of Lesbians and Gays Everywhere) in a letter dated January 1994 and written to *Ten Percent* magazine: "Those of us raised in alternative families, especially lesbian and gay families, have grown up feeling invisible without knowing why. As the next generation grows up, they'll have resources like Newman's book in which they can see themselves reflected and therefore validated."

—Lesléa Newman

A Note on the New Edition

Readers familiar with Heather and her two mommies will notice some changes in the text. The feedback I have received over the past decade from teachers, children's book experts, parents, librarians, child psychologists, and kids has steered me to make several changes in this new anniversary edition. The text is shorter, as I was told many, many times that there were just too many words for children in this age group to listen to. Also, the pages that detail Heather's conception and birth are no longer part of the story. Over the years I have heard from countless parents who wanted to bring Heather into their child's classroom, but were afraid that the explicit explanation of how Heather came to be was a huge deterrent in getting the book read at story time. Many teachers felt the same way. And since omitting those pages did not compromise the story or the message of the book (which is, as Molly tells Heather's classmates and thus children reading the book, "The most important thing about a family is that all the people in it love each other"), I decided to forgo these pages in the hope that Heather, along with her message of respecting and celebrating all types of families, would reach as wide an audience as possible.

—Lesléa Newman